# Affectionate Widow

by

## Joeliah Nabateregga

The Conrad Press

Affectionate Widow

Published by The Conrad Press in the United Kingdom 2023

Tel: +44(0)1227 472 874
www.theconradpress.com
info@theconradpress.com

ISBN 978-1-916966-03-1

Typesetting and Cover Design by: Levellers

The Conrad Press logo was designed by Maria Priestley.

Printed and bound in Great Britain by Clays Ltd, Elcograf S.p.A.

## DEDICATION
I dedicate this book to all widows out there, and to my family and friends


## ACKNOWLEDGEMENT
I thank all those who helped me in this journey of composing this book

# Affectionate Widow

# 1

A small town, Mbiriizi, situated a few miles off the shore of the local river in Lwengo county, Uganda, incubated a lot of good and bad memories. A third of the population in this town were considered nobles as they could afford at least two meals a day.

The town was popularly known for its riverbank best fish sellers, vegetable market vendors, talented football youngsters of the county and strong farmers who supplied almost three quarters of the county with food from their harvest. Overall it was a place of kindhearted and hospitable people.

In that same town, lived the Mukisa family made up of Mr. Jeff Mukisa, Mrs. Pollah Mukisa plus their two children Gabriel and Jevelle.

Mrs. Pollah Mukisa was a retired teacher who had diligently served the community for over twenty years. Kindness flowed in every single bit of word she uttered, this relates to probably why she was referred to as the teacher of the county. Her husband Jeff

Mukisa was a doctor in the county hospital a few blocks from the school she worked in. Gabriel was thirteen while Jevelle was eleven. It was one of the families that anyone would consider happy and indeed they were.

In 2012, during the last month of the dry season, that was a couple of years after Pollah's retirement. She started a youth union as a give back to the society that brought young people together to share ideas on a variety of aspects of life, values and how one should carry oneself in the changing world. It was that same year that brought tragedy to her and from there and then, life was never the same as before.

## 2

Welcome back, Dad,' said Jevelle as she rushed to hug him at the entrance to their home. It was a spacious modern three-bedroom house located on the country side of Lwengo county.

'Thanks,' responded her dad, Jeff Mukisa, as he stood with his arms apart ready to hug up his daughter. They both walked to the dining room.

'Hello darling,' smiled his wife Pollah Mukisa, moving towards the right side of Jeff. Pecked him gently with a kiss.

'Aah,' sighed Jeff as he leant back to the dining table. He asked for dinner since they looked hungry. Pollah rushed to the kitchen to bring food for the family, Jeff helped clearing away all the stuffs on the dining table, spread out the table mats as Pollah brought food for dinner. She had prepared banana commonly known as *matooke*, which is the staple food of Uganda, served with dry fish sauce and French beans.

'Gabriel... Gabriel, where is this little boy?' Jeff asked. Jevelle rushed to Gabriel's room to call on him.

'Wake up, wake up please, Dad is already home,' said Jevelle.

Gabriel responded like he hadn't heard anything to do with sound. Jevelle stood staring at him, she glared up. Gabriel sluggishly tried opening his eyes to peep if anybody was around, unfortunately Jevelle's eyes were as widely open as those of a cat in darkness.

'Ok, let's go,' said Gabriel as he got out of bed. He stretched his arms, organized his trousers and he dropped to the dining room.

'What has made you sleep this early?' asked Jeff.

'I... I was too much tired during the day because... I had too much class work,' replied Gabriel as he squeezed his eyes to put off the blurred vision.

'Let's have supper it's getting late,' said Pollah.

They all sat ready to be served. Jeff put his fork on the table, hauled his plate a little forward, and placed his arms on the dining table with his hands crossed while supporting his chin.

'Any problem, darling?' asked Pollah as she served herself with more dry fish sauce.

'Tomorrow I want to go to Nairobi by air with Gabriel and Jevelle. It's only about forty-five minutes by plane. Are you interested in coming, kids?' asked Jeff.

'Yes!' exclaimed Gabriel.

'Yes, good idea,' said Jevelle as she hurried to go hug his dad.

Jeff asked Pollah to go prepare the stuffs that would be needed for the success of the trip. She packed their clothes, shoes, family Nikon camera, iPads with their respective chargers and included some snacks to eat since they expected a longer waiting before the flight. After supper Pollah went to the kitchen with the used utensils in her hands.

'It's time for bed,' said Jeff.

'Goodnight Mum and Dad,' said Jevelle and Gabriel as they went to their rooms.

12

# 3

O pen the door, darling,' said Pollah as she knocked on Jevelle's door the following morning.

'Come on! It's getting late, get up,' added Pollah standing in the middle of the doorway.

Jevelle greeted Pollah, rushed to the bathroom, showered and dressed quickly. As usual Gabriel was the last in everything at home, again this time round it was him they were waiting for.

At about ten in the morning they set off. Pollah stayed behind as she had to meet with the county youth that evening to run errands in regards to the Youth Union

In the evening after work, she returned home. Alone as she was, she prepared supper and eventually walked towards her bedroom as she passed her fingers in her long hair.

No sooner had she touched the door knob than she heard terrifying news of a plane crash on the television channel since she had forgotten to switch off. It was the very plane that Jeff, Jevelle and Gabriel had taken.

She simply couldn't believe that the plane that had crashed was the very same plane her family had used. She walked slowly towards the television making one step at a time as beads of sweat sprang to her forehead.

No,' she screamed, as tears rolled down her cheeks.

# 4

*Six years later*

Liam, Anita, Sonia, Timothy and Usher were pupils at High Grade Junior School in Masaka. Emerald Kasozi was their favorite teacher despite the fact that she taught them their worst subject which is maths.

Liam Magezi aged thirteen, was shy but always did his best.

Anita Mirembe aged twelve was beautiful, so talkative, social but very stubborn. She made fun of others though she disliked it most. She was the kind of girl who has no permanent seat in class and she liked giving imprudent answers just to attack the class to recognize her presence.

Timothy Kirabo aged thirteen, liked fighting and chaos. He liked teasing other pupils. Timothy was the kind who makes fun for others to guffaw yet he doesn't do it in return. He had a twin brother perhaps that's why he liked company.

Sonia Mulungi aged thirteen, being half African and half Asian, had long brunette hair. She was a positive sort of girl though she easily got snappy.

Usher Mwema aged fourteen, was the cleverest pupil in class, and he used to get the best grades. He was intelligent and often stammered. Fellow pupils made fun of him probably because it's the only weakness he had. He was so insolent, hot tempered with his face always gloomy.

Emerald Kasozi, was their class teacher, she was tall, slender. She was extremely brown that is why many pupils nicknamed her madam white, she was ever smiling and used to put on smartly.

The bell for going home sounded, Sonia rushed to Anita.

'Pick up your books and we hurry home,' Anita stood a bit then picked her bag with books crowding her hands. They both walked together towards the exit.

'Oops!!!' she exclaimed as she hurried back inside to pick her breakfast container.

Sonia stood outside waiting for Anita to return.

'Can we depart now?' asked Sonia

'Yeah,' replied Anita as she nodded her head. Sighed.

Anita seized Sonia's right hand and pulled her while giggling so as to make her move homewards swiftly.

'You are so quick,' said Sonia as she ran and walked in bits with her hair wiggling in the air due to the speed.

'Good bye, remember your homework,' said Anita as she crossed the road leading to their home.

Sonia's home was a bit far from Anita's. Despite her home being near, Anita reached home last. Guess where she spent most of her time. Anita on her way, she passed by the house of Pollah the widow whose family passed on in a plane crash. Pollah and Anita's mother Holly were not only neighbors but also great friends. Every after classes, Anita passed via this widow's home. She spent most of her time there. The widow would narrate stories to her, play with her, give her good dolls, read for her favorite books. Pollah did all that was missing in Anita's life since her mother was always caught up with garden work.

'Welcome back dear,' giggled Pollah as she welcomed Anita into her palatial home and embraced her. Anita often went to see Pollah when she came home from school. The widow's house was a bit distant from other neighbors in the vicinity, this gave Anita time to enjoy with her without any disturbance.

Pollah gave Anita a glass of red juice and some potato chips, she started drinking, having taken half of it, she rotated her eyes around just searching for a clock to see what the time was.

'Oh my God! It's getting late mum will be mad at me,' said Anita as she swiftly picked up her bag and books then she ran as fast as her legs could hold her out of Pollah's compound. Breathing space was only after she reached their home.

'Mum... mum... mum,' she called loudly tiptoeing and peeping into the house. The whole place seemed blank.

She whizzed behind the house through the back door just thinking on where her mother was.

'Anita,' her mother called out to direct her on where she was. Anita with her bag on the back ran to the orchard only to see her mother busy watering the flowers.

Anita's mother gently kissed Anita's forehead.

'Welcome back,' said Anita's mother.

'First go change into your casual clothes then we shall chat more,' she added with a watering can in her hands.

17

# 5

'Good morning class,' Emerald said to them, her arms folded behind her body.

'Good morning madam,' replied the whole class as they all stood up.

'Excuse me Timothy, why are you bending down?' asked the teacher as she stretched her neck to see what the matter was with Timothy.

'No... it's... it... it's just that I had dropped my pen as I was getting to my feet,' stammered Timothy.

'Ok take your seats class,' they all sat down.

'Usher tell us, where did we get to in our last maths lesson?' asked Emerald.

'Www...we got to...multi... tii... plication,' stammered Usher and looked around.

Almost all the pupils burst into laughter since they couldn't believe that he had all that time just speaking out only four word (we stopped on multiplication).

'Let's leave that, thanks Usher,' said the teacher as she used her hands to make the class silent.

'12 X 3...,' wrote Emerald on the chalkboard.

'Liam come help solve this for the class,' she asked.

Liam looked blank, not believing his ears that he was called upon to find a solution for the problem.

'Liam come on,' added Emerald.

The whole class turned their heads behind just to see if anybody named Liam would try coming up.

'Liam stand up please,' whispered Enock who sat next to Liam on his right-hand side.

Liam stood up, went to the chalkboard. He walked slowly as he shied away busy removing dirt from his fingernails although nothing was there grimy.

He reached the front, facing the board, with his back facing the class, head bent forward and downwards with his fingers twisting the piece of chalk in his hands.

'Please write the answer,' said Emerald as she moved slowly towards the back of the classroom audience.

Liam lifted his arm, placed it on the chalkboard with his head still bent. He eventually wrote the answer '18' with his fingers still holding the chalk yet shadowing the answer.

'Please put your hand off for the class to see the answer,' said the teacher.

'Class, is it correct?' Emerald asked.

'No,' replied the class in a sharp uniform voice as Usher rose his hand up to volunteer.

'Usher go solve it for us, Liam come back to your seat but be attentive please,' she added.

Usher moved to the front as Liam moved to the back of the class. He wrote the answer and he confidently walked back to his seat.

'Thank you, Usher,' giggled Emerald. The class clapped sharply appreciating Usher for the good job done. The teacher continued until the last bit of her teaching session.

'We are to have a test next week, please prepare adequately, remember whoever fails it will be demoted,' said the teacher at the end of the lesson.

'Have a nice time,' she added as she picked up her text book and left the class.

The bell sounded and the pupils moved out for break.

# 6

Oh my God, Maths again,' sighed Timothy. 'Look at me, poor at Maths, a test and then demotion. This is serious,' Sonia explained to Anita in total perplexity.

Liam never moved out. He stayed inside the classroom thinking about the recent scenario, the upcoming test and the penalty attached to its failure. He placed his arms on the desk, bent the head with his face facing downwards.

'Liam, get up,' said Anita as she forced Liam's head upwards. She moved round and sat next to him on his right-hand side. She crossed her arm over Liam's back in a comforting manner.

'You can do it next time, Liam,' she added as she pulled her eyebrows up.

'I have failed again, Anita,' said Liam with his eyes becoming watery.

Usher came in, came closer to where Anita and Liam were sitting.

'Hmmm uuu you aah are a... real cow...coward. How ca... can that mak...e you crr...y?' said Usher moving towards his seat wondering and having beats of smiles.

Anita felt touched about Liam's state of sadness. She rushed to Usher in a way that shows desire to speak angrily.

'Usher,' Anita called out angrily while pinpointing at him. She then moved away and went back to where Liam was sitting.

Anita as usual, she went to Pollah's home and this time she was so far different from her normal. She looked puzzled, tired, sunk in thoughts and having poverty of speech.

'What is it, darling?' asked Pollah.

'Aaa... aa, it's nothing' replied Anita as she passed her hand in her hair.

'Do not lie Anita, please tell me what the matter is,' the widow asked again.

'Ok, it's just that my friend is upset because he does no well in class,' replied Anita.

'Oh, sorry to hear that,' said Pollah as she brought Anita to her closest.

'I have to go home early today,' said Anita with her head in Pollah's chest.

'It's all right, darling,' replied Pollah.

'Bye, Aunt Pollah,' said Anita. She waved as she left the compound.

'Liam son, welcome back,' said Elsy Liam's mother as she welcomed his son inside their bungalow.

'I'm ok, Mummy,' replied Liam in a very low tone.

'I can tell something is bothering you, tell me what the matter is son,' added Elsy. She gently touched Liam's shoulders.

'Mother, it's about school,' replied Liam.

'So, you are playing again?' asked Liam's mother nastily as she stood up pointing at him.

Liam knew he had messed up by notifying his mother about the bad news as his mother had promised to take him back to his drunkard father who used to beat him daily if he failed any test again. Liam's mother was so catatonic that she even never gave Liam a chance to talk about any problem affecting him more but caning him severely in case he failed a test. Liam moved to his room, closed the door and leant on it with his head facing upwards.

'Oh God, this stuff again!' exclaimed Liam as he fell on his bed by the back.

# 7

Monday morning, it was the midterm test week. All the pupils we full of apprehension on how the test would be, the content in the test and also what literally was to be done to score highly. Timothy and his neighbor Mariam were seen whispering to each other in a puzzled state.

'I hope it's nice and easy with lots of adding rather than multiplication,' said Sonia as she placed her right-hand palm to support her cheek.

'Please get in order in class and take your seats,' said Emerald with test papers in her right hand.

The pupils moved their chairs.

'Usher please distribute these papers to the class,' said the teacher. Usher moved forward towards her to pick the test papers.

He distributed them and returned the excess to the teacher.

'Start, it's 8:00am and by... (she looks at her wrist watch) by 10:00am everybody should be through,' said Emerald. She quickly moved out smartly to go to the staff room.

'This is a real mess,' whispered Timothy to Liam with his eyes widely open.

'Uhm, let's do the test time is against us, the teacher may find us talking and she will disqualify us,' said Liam as he placed he hand holding the pen in the test paper.

The whole class was as mute as a grave, every pupil's head was facing into the test paper.

'it's one hour left,' said Emerald as soon as she reached the classroom entrance.

'Excuse me,' said Anita as she raised her arm for more answer booklets.

The whole class turned their heads to the left to see who was asking for more. Anita's eyes met with those of Liam and they both smiled.

Liam was comfortably seated with only two questions answered on the test paper, that was his name and the 3+6 question which was number four in section A.

'it's time, stand up and hand in please,' said the teacher with her hands widely open ready to receive the test papers.

As always Usher was the first pupil to hand in and he moved out, after two more minutes, Anita handed in too. Timothy followed, Sonia and other pupils too handed in Liam exclusive.

'Liam won't you hand in?' asked the teacher with an affirmative face.

Liam stood up and moved towards the teacher. Emerald opened Liam's test paper only to find out that he had answered nothing.

'What's this?' asked the teacher with Liam's paper in her hands.

Liam looked downwards, a lot of pupils were peeping through the classroom window trying to figure out what might be happening inside. Anita too was there watching everything. She pitied her friend.

'Let's go to the staff room perhaps it's from there that you will be able to complete the test,' said Emerald furiously. She walked quickly as Liam followed back to face. On reaching the staff room, Liam stood next to the third chair right from the staff table.

'So, are you willing to complete my test?' asked Emerald. Pulled her eyebrows up.

'Yes teacher,' replied Liam with a timid broken voice.

Liam sat down in the chair, his paper on the staffroom table. He started filling the blank spaces in the test paper though unaware of what exactly was to be filled. A few minutes Liam returned the test paper after answering what only his mind would remember.

# 8

**M**other we had a math test today,' said Timothy while standing in front of his mother Hazel.

'How are your expectations son?' asked Hazel, Timothy's mother.

'Mother am hungry,' said Timothy trying to dodge her mother's question since things out of the test never worked out well.

'So, are you not going to answer my question?' asked Hazel

'Mum, please let's talk about this when the results are back,' said Timothy. Rushed to his room with his bag in the hands.

'May I come in?' asked Anita as she knocked on Pollah's front door, she opened it and glanced at Pollah lying in the sofa with her head raised on the sofa pillows.

'You are welcome, as she lifted her legs from the sofa so as to sit upright,' said Pollah.

'Any good news for me?' she asked.

'Not really, we just had a Maths test at school,' replied Anita.

'How was it? 'asked Pollah.

'I will be honest with you, it was hard and you know I am not good at Maths,' replied Anita.

'Well, I hope one day my Maths grades will get better,' she added.

Pollah narrated to her the story of her late son Gabriel who had the same issue with Maths.

'So, then how did he manage getting good grades?' asked Anita with a very curious face.

'I did and my late husband too helped at times,' said Pollah as she passed her fingers in Anita's hair.

'It took a while but eventually his grades got better,' She added.

'Wow so... so, can you help me also? 'asked Anita as she looked downwards. Looked diffident.

'(Smiles), I will my daughter Jevelle oh! sorry I meant Anita,' the widow answered as she passed her arm around Anita's back of neck.

# 9

A week later after the test, the teacher walked to class with the results from the test she had given a week ago.

'Almost half of the class failed last week's test,' said Emerald as she slowly walked around the class.

'I am returning your papers so that we can make corrections,' she added.

She commenced calling out names on the test papers starting with the best performers. Liam was read last. Emerald asked him to come along with his mother the following week to discuss his performance needs.

Liam couldn't believe his ears because he could picture her mother's reaction in case he told her what the teacher had said. Anita looked back at him in a very pathetic manner.

'Mum will punish me for this, she is so hard on me,' said Liam with tear drops rolling down his cheeks.

'No, Liam don't say that,' said Anita as she embraced him.

'All is well,' she added.

'So, what are you going to do?' asked Anita in total perplexity.

'Am not going back home Ani... (cries), I cannot fa... face mummy,' said Liam as he burst into tears.

'All right don't cry friend, I have a plan,' said Anita as she wiped off Liam's tears.

Together they walked towards Pollah's house. Discussed much, all the way to her home all in essence of figuring how things are going to work out in favor of Liam.

They got to Pollah's compound with Liam walking just behind after Anita.

'This is my friend Liam, the one I told you about the last time we talked,' said Anita as she introduced Liam to Pollah

'Come on Liam,' said Pollah with her hands widely open to hug him.

'You look sad, did anything happen on the way?' asked Pollah.

Liam was as silent as a grave with his face facing downwards.

'Tell me son,' added the Pollah.

Liam's eyes became watery. Pollah perceived it that something was not adding up, she paused asking then she brought him closer to her chest.

'Sorry son,' said Pollah in much agony with her cheek placed on Liam's head.

'He failed the test and the teacher sent for his mother,' Anita hurried in to speak.

'Is he going to explain it to her mother?' Pollah asked.

'No... no!!!' defended Anita.

'Mummy iii... ss will beat me...,' cried out Liam.

'Stop crying darling, I will try talking to your teacher,' said Pollah. Passed her palms on Liam's cheeks

'Uhm, can ca... can you...?' stammered Anita.

'Pardon me darling,' said Pollah.

'Can you go to school in place of Liam's mother?' pardoned Anita.

'Are you serious!' exclaimed Pollah. Smiled broadly

'Liam would you accept that?' asked Anita with a deep look at Liam.

'Of courses yes, because I am worried about mum getting to know about this, she will obviously cain me,' replied Liam.

'Ok, I will give it a though kids,' said the widow. She hugged them together.

# 10

What is wrong as you are mute today?' Sonia asked Anita.

'I am fine, I just want some time alone,' responded Anita. Looked serious.

'Is Liam bringing his mother?' asked one of the pupils at the back of the class.

'No, she can't, Liam's mother is extremely harsh, she might have beaten him.' answered Timothy as he stood up to peep outside through the window.

*A week later.*

'Isn't that Liam and his mother?' asked Sonia as she pointed at Liam and Pollah at the office entrance.

They entered the office.

'Good morning?' Emerald greeted both Liam and Pollah as they set their first feet into the office.

'Please have a seat,' she added as she used her hands to locate the seats. She as well reached for a chair.

'Have we met before?' Emerald continued to ask.

'Your face looks familiar,' she added with a curious face as she gently stroked her pen on her left cheek.

'I used to work here before my retirement, that was some good years ago, my husband too used to cover at the school clinic as the doctor on call,' Pollah answered. Secured her handbag on the laps.

'I am Liam's aunt,' she added with Liam's hands locked in hers

'Liam told me the whole story about the test,' added Pollah confidently.

'Yes, you are right, I suggest he should either be demoted or repeat the class as a way of allowing him to reflect on all that has been taught in this academic year,' replied the teacher as she looked at Liam.

'Liam needs more support and time,' she added.

'What if we pardon Liam? His grade will get better I believe,' pleaded Pollah.

'Liam is not one of the industrious pupils that we can count on, even a second chance may fail us,' said Emerald as she placed school text books in the drawer of the side cabinet

'Kindly take my word, there is room for change if a chance is granted. I will make efforts to see to it that he improves his grades,' Pollah said with a pleading face.

'Ok, Liam it is up to you to prove that you are worthy a second chance,' the teacher added pointing at him.

'I promise to do my best Aunt Pollah and Madam Emerald,' said Liam with his eyes filled with tears.

'I swear upon the Lord,' he added with his palms together.

'Thanks Emerald for your time,' said Pollah as she giggled. They all smiled.

'Welcome,' replied Emerald.

Liam and Pollah moved out of the office, stood outside and they were seen discussing.

'Thanks Aunt Pollah,' said Liam as he deflexed his head to look into Pollah's face.

The rest of the pupils were eagerly peeping through the windows looking forward to hearing what the decision was from Emerald.

'Please proceed to class,' said Pollah.

'See you soon, perhaps later in the evening,' Liam said. Waved at Pollah and proceeded to class.

'What did she say? Are you demoted? Has she pardoned you? Tell me please,' asked Anita incoherently and pressured.

'I will elucidate all to you Anita, let's go sit down,' responded Liam as they all moved towards their seats.

'I guess Liam was not demoted!' exclaimed Timothy.

'Aaaa... I cac... can't tee... ll,' stammered Usher.

Both Timothy and Sonia moved towards Liam, asked him all that had transpired from the meeting with Emerald.

Liam informed them he was granted a second chance to make things right.

'Who was that woman?' asked Timothy.

'She is my aunt, Aunt Pollah,' replied Liam as she looked straight into Timothy's eyes.

'Does your mother know about this?' asked Sonia.

'No, I never told her, guess what she would do,' replied Liam as he turned his head to Sonia.

'Better that I am free again,' he added. Sighed.

That is great Liam although you have to go an extra mile in calculating maths numbers because we need you buddy,' said Timothy. Gently patting on Liam's back and they both smiled.

Liam's life was renewed. Anita was seen moving closer to Liam.

The bell for going back home sounded. All the pupils rushed to pick up their bags and departed.

'Oh, today is a remarkable day,' Liam sighed while putting his bag on the back.

'Thank God Madam white accepted Pollah's proposal,' said Anita as they all moved out of the school gate.

'Let's go meet her, I mean Aunt Mukisa,' said Liam blissfully.

'You now call her aunt?' asked Anita as she stopped walking. Smiled.

'Yes, is it bad? She deserves it.' said Liam. They both laughed.

## 11

How was school?' asked Pollah. 'To me, school was more like a miracle today,' Liam said. Pulled off his bag from the back.

'Thanks once again Aunt Pollah,' said Liam humbly.

'All right, let's go to the dinning room, I prepared something for you,' said the widow. Opened her hands directing them where the dining room was.

They both moved together to the dining room.

'My favorite food,' said Anita as she reached for a chair.

Pollah had prepared smashed potato with mushroom soup.

Liam was asked to recite a prayer before they ate.

After the prayer, they all ate then moved to the sitting room when food was done.

'Who are those in the photo? They look smart,' asked Liam pointing at the framed photo on the wall.

'(bits of silence) They were my children,' replied Pollah as she reached for the photo on the wall. She gently wiped off the dust from the frame that had spread.

'What happened to them? Are they in Paris?' asked Anita as she requested for the photo to observe more.

'Why Paris, is it because you have dreams of reaching there?' asked Liam. Laughed making fun of Anita.

'This was my daughter Jevelle and my son Gabriel,' responded Pollah in a low tone as she used her finger to locate the photos

'They would be as old as you are now, they passed on in a plane crash few years back as they were traveling for a trip with their dad,' she added.

'I loved them so much and I miss them always,' said as she hugged the photo frame.

There was a lot of silence in the room, only to hear the sound of the shouting kids from the neighborhood.

'Sorry about that Aunt Pollah,' said Anita as she gently touched Pollah's hands.

'We would have been friends with them, I would have played football with Gabriel,' Liam said with a broad smile on his face.

'We have to leave for home,' said Anita.

'You are right, it's getting late,' Liam added.

'You are always welcome anytime you feel like coming back here,' said Pollah. Sighed.

Pollah escorted Anita and Liam to the home gate. They waved to each other as they all went to their respective homes.

'Are the tests results out?' asked Liam's mother.

'(silence) yes mother,' replied Liam.

'Please get yourself something to eat,' said Elsy, Liam's mother. Moved to her room.

# 12

A week later, Liam went back to Pollah's house. Liam asked Pollah if she could help him with daily maths coaching lessons. Fortunately she accepted.

'If it's for your academic excellence darling, then I will have to do it,' replied Pollah.

Anita never knew about this. Liam started going to the widow's home daily every evening for coaching lessons.

Pollah taught him variety of things, he learnt addition, subtraction, multiplication, division and the multiplication table that used to challenge almost all the pupils in class.

Liam learnt many things in maths. She taught him topics that were far not yet covered in class. On top of that, Liam asked Pollah to stretch her helping hand in all other subjects too. She did all that was possible to change Liam's grades. Pollah not only taught Liam things to do with books but also good morals, values of life and how he should carry himself around people. She treated him like her own son.

'Good afternoon class,' greeted Emerald

'We are fine, thank you madam Emerald,' replied the pupils.

Emerald introduced a new sub topic which was the Lowest Common Multiple (LCM) and Greatest Common Factor (GCF) of numbers. Almost the whole class had never heard of this before.

'Anybody with an idea on this?' asked the teacher.

The class was like nobody knows. As silent as a grave.

'What is the lowest common multiple of 6 and 9?' wrote Emerald.

'No trial again?' she asked the class.

'I can try teacher,' Liam said. For the first time since the start of the term. He all looked confident.

'You Liam! You mean about what we are discussing today or you have other business to say?' exclaimed Emerald. She smiled.

A very indescribable sound was heard in the class. The murmuring increased moment by moment. Each and every pupil looked shocked. They couldn't believe that even Usher the cleverest pupil in class had no idea on the question written on board.

'Come over Liam,' said the teacher. She gave him a piece of chalk.

Liam confidently moved to the front to answer the question. He stood with his hand on the chalkboard.

He looked like he was memorizing what Pollah had taught him.

He started calculating the number, he patently and tidily showed every bit of step he used till he came to the final answer. The whole class was quite just looking forward to seeing the nonsense Liam was going to write down.

'I am done,' said Liam giving back the piece of chalk to Emerald.

'Clap for Liam,' said Emerald.

Liam couldn't believe that he had made it. He couldn't believe that the clapping applause from the pupils was a sign of appreciation towards him.

'Yes,' whispered Liam as he boxed the air.

The whole class was horrified.

'How did he even do it?' whispered Usher to Timothy.

'Who taught you this Liam?' asked Emerald. She requested Liam to stand up and tell the rest of the class.

'It was all my research work,' replied Liam as he smiled.

Emerald asked the class to do the same as Liam. She told all the pupils to consult Liam so that he could share with them on how he managed to do it. Liam had done literally what the teacher was to teach in that session.

'Have a nice afternoon,' said the teacher as she moved out of the class.

'Tell me the secret Liam, did you copy from the teacher's text book?' Anita asked as she laughed in total suspense.

'No, my dear, how dare?' replied Liam. Smiled

Almost all the pupils consulted Liam as the teacher had instructed. Liam helped all those who went to him apart from Usher who never bothered. Usher thought of it as being vulnerable. He was seen sitting at the back of the class deeply sunk in thoughts.

'Can I help you too?' Liam asked Usher.

'No, I need nothing from you poor boy,' Usher replied stubbornly. Moved out of the class furiously.

Liam turned his head and looked at him as he walked out of his sight.

'So, I did wrong?' Liam whispered to himself.

For the first time Liam was happy. He kept smiling at everyone he met on the school compound.

The following day, Emerald came to class. She asked if everyone had consulted Liam.

'What is the Lowest Common Multiple of 4 and 12?' wrote the teacher.

She asked if anyone can help solve the question. Usher moved to go solve it. He gave the answer as 6. He did this intending to prove a point to Liam.

'It's wrong, usher,' said the teacher. She moved in front of the class.

'Did you go to Liam for help?' Emerald asked.

Usher had no answer to that question. He just looked down on the floor. The whole class never thought of Usher failing any maths question.

'No!' said Usher to himself. Looked ashamed. Usher felt very small. He felt like all that was his had been taken.

The teacher called upon Liam to correct Usher by working it out for the class.

'Thanks Liam,' added the teacher. Emerald taught more and more. Many pupils came up front to solve the questions as Liam was alternatively called upon to correct until the session was done.

'Thanks for being active pupils, do the homework I have left behind,' the teacher said.

'Liam follow me to my office now,' she added.

Liam followed Emerald. He went thinking of what the teacher was going to say to him this time round. He remembered the last time he was called, things didn't turn out well.

'What again?' wondered in a very low whisper.

They entered the office together.

'Have a seat please,' said Emerald.

'Thanks teacher,' responded Liam as he reached for a seat.

He looked paranoid, and nervous on what was next.

'Do not be afraid Liam, nothing to worry about,' said the teacher to alley his anxiety. Placed her arms on the office table.

'Aaaahh… Liam every teacher is literally amused by your classroom involvement lately, you have drastically and positively changed, everything about you seems different,' said Emerald.

'Tell me, what is the secret, Liam?' added the teacher.

'Sighed Liam, nothing much teacher, just that aunt Pollah coaches me in math every evening,' he said. Shied away.

'Then that's great, Liam, your transformation is making everyone delighted,' the teacher said.

'That's all I had to ask and longing to know, please you can now return to class,' concluded Emerald.

Liam returned to class, walked directly to his seat with every pupil giving him a strong stare.

# 13

'I thank God school is getting more interesting,' said Liam to Pollah.

'Can you believe I answered the maths question which even Usher the cleverest pupil in class failed!' exclaimed Liam.

'Haha... yes, no more plunging. Teach me more and more Aunt 6Pollah,' added Liam blissfully. Picked up his books eager to learn more.

'Mummy good evening,' greeted Liam in amazement.

'You seem very amused and jolly son,' replied Liam's mother with an astonished look.

'Mum school is very enjoyable, more than words could explain, speak to you later let me first attend to my homework,' said Liam.

Liam's mother was astonished and left in a bit of shock. She wondered what had transformed her son's customs.

She reminded Liam of the olden days who never reminded himself about homework, who used to wail when told to do so. She was really perplexed about what his son might have turned into.

Liam had wholly changed, he no more waited for his mother to wake him up for school as it was previously.

'Liam darling its school time, wake up,' said Elsy. Opened the door only to find out that Liam was nowhere to be found. She glanced at where Liam usually puts his bag and uniform, the place was blank. She checked her wrist watch.

'What! My goodness!' she exclaimed.

'It is 7:02am,' she added as she closed the door on Liam's room and rushed to the home compound.

Liam woke up early to go meet Pollah. Unfortunately, he found her with a terrible headache.

'Oh dear,' said Liam placing his palm on Pollah's forehead.

Liam looked distressed, he comforted Pollah as much as he could, put a cold compress on where the head ached most and he also gave her water to take medicine.

'Take this, you will soon be fine,' said Liam sitting on the edge of Pollah's bed.

'Won't you attend school today?' asked Pollah with a low-pitched voice.

'Oh gosh! It's clocking 8:30am,' exclaimed Liam as he stared at the clock. He swiftly ran to school as he was already late.

'Where is Liam?' the teacher asked.

All the pupils turned to Liam's seat, regrettably he was not there. Suddenly a voice from the entrance was heard. It was Liam asking for permission to get into the classroom.

'Come in right here,' yelled Emerald their maths teacher.

'Where are you from? Why are you late? What is the time?' asked the teacher pressuredly.

Liam looked blank, he had nothing to say.

'I waa i wa… as… with…,' stammered Liam.

'I beg your pardon, with who,' added the teacher angrily.

Liam rolled his eyes to the class only to find out that all the eyes were on him waiting on what was coming out of his conscious.

'My Aunt is sick. I had to first attend to her,' answered Liam.

'Ok, but let this not happen again Liam, go sit down,' said Emerald. Liam walked straight to his seat.

The teacher taught but Liam looked absent minded, his mind was far away from class. He was thinking of his sick friend Pollah. He all looked anxious and stressed.

'What would be the problem?' Liam whispered to himself. He frequently sighed just stuck on what to do next. All the pupils moved out of the class after the session but Liam kept still in his seat.

'Liam are you serious, is Aunt Pollah sick?' asked Anita as she rushed to where Liam was sitting.

'Yes Anita, she is seriously ill,' replied Liam. He anteverted his head.

(Bits of silence)

We should go visit her later this evening,' Anita suggested.

'That will be lovely indeed,' said Liam. Placed his hands on the head. He all looked puzzled

'You shouldn't worry so much Liam,' Anita said. She passed her hand around Liam's neck in a comforting manner.

'I am scared, she may die Anita,' said Liam. His eyes filled up with tears. He felt helpless with much pity inside him.

'No don't say that Liam, be positive dude,' answered Anita.

They both left class for breakfast, moved silently without any conversation between them. Liam was full of apprehension the entire day.

'Do you mean the woman you came with last time?' Timothy asked.

'You are right, buddy,' replied Liam.

Timothy consoled his friend.

When it was time to go home, Liam rushed to pick his bag

'Let's hurry, Anita,' said Liam as they rushed to Pollah's house.

'Anita I can't imagine my life if anything terrible happens to Aunt Pollah,' Liam added as he made small steps. Anita just looked and gave no answer.

In a blink of an eye, they were in the widow's compound. The whole place was as silent as a grave, it felt like a deserted country house.

'Pollah,' called Liam knocking on the door to Pollah's bedroom.

They both entered the room.

'Oh, Anita you visited once again. It has been a while since you last came here,' said Pollah. Giggled.

'Come on kids,' she added as she opened her arms to hug them.

They both climbed her bed with each of them going either side of Pollah, Liam on the right and Anita on the left. They leant their heads on her shoulders.

'How do you feel?' Liam asked.

'Liam was worried the entire day. He couldn't concentrate in class,' Anita rushed in to speak.

'You shouldn't worry about me, I will definitely get well,' Pollah said.

'Let's go to the dining room, I prepared something for you,' she added.

'Aunt Pollah why? What if you hurt yourself? what if you burnt yourself? Don't you know that your seriously ill and weak?' asked Liam in total perplexity.

They all moved slowly to the dining room. Pollah had prepared fried rice with meat sauce.

'Aunt Pollah allow me to serve you today please,' Anita said as she reached for a plate. She served all of them.

After the meal, Pollah asked the kids to go home as early as they could. Liam never wanted to leave he insisted on staying.

Anita tried persuading him but all in vain, he never wanted to leave Pollah by herself. He started crying.

'I will tell mummy about you and I will request her to allow me look after you till when you get better,' Liam said. Tears rolling down his cheeks.

'Its all right darling, no need to cry,' said Pollah. She wiped Liam's tears as she comforted him.

Pollah walked them to the main exit. She couldn't walk any further since she was still lethargic. They all waved at Pollah as she also waved back and they walked home.

Liam reached home, he was so quiet.

'What is the matter, son?' asked Elsy Liam's mother as he tried to find out what was wrong with his son.

Liam narrated to her mother everything about Pollah and how sick she was.

'She is a good person, Mum, Anita introduced her to me,' Liam explained

'I just don't want to see my friends sick, it makes me hel... pp... less,' added Liam as he burst into tears.

Elsy pitied both Liam and the widow.

'Come closer darling, all is well son,' Elsy said as she hugged Liam

Liam declined supper, all he did was think himself to sleep. He was never in such a state before.

Despite the fact that Liam was a little boy, he cared much more like an adult.

Just like the previous morning, Liam woke up very early and went to meet Pollah. This time round he managed to catch up with time. He assisted the widow with medicine and he then departed for school on time.

'I wish I was a doctor,' said Liam to Anita and Sonia.

'My dad wants me to become a doctor when I grow up,' added Sonia. They all smiled

Later in the evening, Liam and Anita went to check on Pollah. Her condition was better and promising. They did that for the next six days till Pollah fully recovered.

The bond between these three grew stronger each day that passed.

# 14

Five weeks later, a test was done again. Results were out and Liam was among the best three students.

All the teachers were surprised on seeing Liam's academic improvement. Usher as always, he emerged as the top best pupil with Liam being third.

Liam never stop reading hard and seeking help from Pollah. He impressed all the teachers because of his great improvement. Pollah too was impressed

'Thanks Liam for being industrious,' said Elsy as she looked through the test result card.

'You are welcome, Mother,' replied Liam. Smiled broadly.

Liam's mother had no idea that it was Pollah who helped Liam change his grades. She thought maybe Liam was giving more time to his books than he used to.

'If dad gets to know about this, he won't beat me again and he will also stop taking alcohol,' said Liam blissfully.

His mother hugged him tightly. She couldn't believe the words her son had uttered.

Going back to school almost all the pupils started befriending Liam. Many wanted to be helped in different subjects more so maths. Liam's good manners at school earned him as many friends as infinite.

Sonia and Timothy too asked Liam to support them so they could change their grades although they weren't as badly off as Liam was before.

'Liam tell us, will you also help us?' asked Sonia and Timothy.

'Why not my dear ones?' replied Liam as he smiled

Not like Usher, Liam accepted to assist every pupil who asked for his support.

'Liam what is the secret to this good performance in class,' asked Sonia and Timothy

He told them it was Aunt Pollah helping him out.

'Can he do the same for us too' Sonia and Timothy asked Liam. Sonia shied away

'It's upon her to decide, I can't speak on her behalf,' replied Liam

'I will probably speak to her and see what she will say,' he added

They all smiled and moved back to class.

That very evening, Liam went to Pollah's house. He explained to her what his friends had asked. Pollah without hesitation, she accepted their request.

'Thanks, Pollah for that good heart, 'Liam thanked the widow.

'It's no big deal,' replied the widow. They both hugged.

The following day, Sonia and Timothy were eager to know what Pollah had said to Liam.

'Did you tell her?' asked Timothy.

'What did she say?' Sonia hurried in to ask too.

'She accepted,' responded Liam.

'Where and when shall we meet her?' Timothy asked with excitement.

'As soon as you guys are ready, we will have to meet her at her house,' Liam answered

'Its just few blocks from here,' he added

'I can't wait to start,' Timothy said as he jumped up. Boxed the air

'You are not saying anything,' Timothy asked Sonia

'it… it is just that… iii…,' stammered Sonia.

'Speak up Sonia,' Timothy hurried in to speak.

'My mother warned me about going to strangers' houses,' Sonia said with a worried look on her face as she squeezed her fingernails

'Come-on Sonia, the person we are talking about is Liam's aunt,' Timothy said.

'Look Sonia, there is nothing to worry about, she can't cause any harm to us,' Liam added as he brought Sonia closer to his right side.

'I trust you Liam, I will come with you in the evening,' Sonia said. Smiled

When the bell was sounded, Timothy rushed to where Liam was seated so they would go to Pollah's house.

'Let me finish my work first,' Liam replied.

After his class work, the group moved to Pollah's house. Anita too came along.

They walked conversing and laughing all through the way.

'Can we come in?' Liam asked as he knocked on the door.

'Oh, you are here already,' said Pollah as she welcomed them into the house. Smiled.

Liam and Anita entered first because they were well conversant with the house. Sonia entered last in a peeping manner. They sat down in the sitting room.

Sonia was so mute like she had been warned over talking.

'Aunt Pollah, please meet Sonia and Timothy our classmates,' Liam said.

'Timothy and Sonia, this is Aunt Pollah the one I told you about,' he added. They all smiled.

'Say something Sonia,' said Liam as he gently pulled Sonia's hand.

'I am fine Liam,' replied Sonia politely

Pollah commenced the group discussion. They all actively participated and indeed a lot was discussed.

After the session, Pollah served them with orange juice and asked them to go home safely.

'Thanks, Pollah,' they all said in a group. Smiled to each other.

'Can we come back tomorrow?' Sonia asked.

'Of course, I will be waiting for you every single day,' replied Pollah.

They all walked to their respective homes happily. Timothy could not stop revising what was discussed that very evening.

'Mum I got a new teacher,' said Timothy.

'Is she new at school?' asked Hazel Timothy's mother.

'No, she is Mrs... (tried memorizing the name) ya... yeah Pollah my new friend,' answered Timothy happily.

'So where does she live?' asked Hazel.

'A few miles from here, closer to school,' replied Timothy.

'Ok, please get yourself something to drink from the fridge,' concluded Hazel

The same conversation was held at Sonia's home where she told Gianne her mother about the new friend who was also a teacher. Sonia's mother looked comfortable with the point although she still remained Sonia to keep safe around strangers.

'Make sure you have someone with you every time you visit her house,' said Gianne.

'Exactly mother,' replied Sonia.

Liam, Anita, Sonia and Timothy spent most of their evenings at the widow's place. They became part of the widow. She taught them different things like bathing, doing house work, playing musical instruments.

School life of the four pupils greatly changed, their discipline too improved. They became great friends who learnt to work together, they attended class more than any other pupil.

'Why are you not in your seats?' asked Mr. Heizer Kagame there English teacher.

'I feel more comfortable sitting here,' answered Timothy.

These good four friends had switched their back seats with those that belonged to the pupils who sat in the front. The teacher was surprised with the new sitting arrangement in class.

Guess where the pupils who used to sit on the front seats were? Liam had promised to help them with classwork daily if they gave up the seats which they willingly did.

'So, are you sitting in front for today or forever?' asked the Mr. Heizer Kagame.

'Always and forever teacher,' replied the four friends. Bits of laughter were heard from the back of the class.

Usher wasn't pleased at all, He was seen in the middle column of the class mumbling.

As soon as the teacher left the class after the session, Usher rushed angrily to where the four friends were sitting.

'How dare you?' Usher demanded furiously.

'What is your problem?' Sonia asked.

'Uuu... you cch... chased your fee... fellow pu... pils from the fff... front seats,' Usher stammered angrily.

'Hahaha,' Timothy guffawed.

'Why are you the one complaining and not them?' added Timothy.

'Chill little boy,' Anita added.

They all walked out of the class leaving Usher alone. The entire class was aware of Usher's bad manners and the way he treated each and everyone just because he was the class's best performer. Usher persistently mocked and insulted a lot of his classmates reminding them of how dull they were. This left Usher with no friends as no one would want to relate with someone of his kind. Usher was jealous because of these four friends.

'I have to put a stop on this,' Usher said as he banged the desk. He gently nodded his head. Usher planned on ruining the friendship between Anita, Sonia, Liam and Timothy. He tried several tricks multiple times but he never succeeded

## 15

*Two weeks later*

Monday morning, Usher came to class very early. Hardly had he entered classroom when the four good friends came in. They sat and got their story books to read. Usher had a plan in mind. He came to where they were sitting.

'Don't come near us,' Sonia shouted at Usher. Pushed him.

'Stop it Sonia, allow him to say what he wants to say and then depart,' Liam said as he held Sonia's hand. Sonia geared.

'Remember Aunt Pollah said violence is not always the answer,' Liam added.

'Have you gone to the office? Madam Emerald called for all of you,' said Usher confidently.

'Go check what she might be saying,' added Usher.

'Get off our way,' Sonia said. Pushed Usher out of the way.

They all walked to the office happily not knowing Usher was tricking them.

As soon as they moved out of the classroom, Usher rushed to his school bag, grabbed his English text book pushed it into Liam's school bag, removed his wrist watch and placed it into Sonia's bag too. He then swiftly rushed back to his seat. Looked like nothing had happened.

'You lied to us?' said Anita as soon as they returned from the staff room.

'No, ma... ma.... y be thee....te te...teacher ha has gone so... so somewhere,' stammered Usher.

'Forget it, let's resume reading,' Liam replied politely. They all walked to their respective seats.

Pupils were still arriving for school for it was clocking 8:30am.

Usher peeped through the window, when he saw that their science teacher was heading to class, he placed his head on the desk with his face facing downwards in the essence of pretending to sleep.

'Good morning Madam Monalisa,' said the pupils as they stood up to welcome the teacher. Usher remained sitting with his head still placed on the desk.

'Usher, why are you sleeping at this hour of the morning?' asked Monalisa.

'Aaa... am not o... ok,' replied Usher as he sat upright.

'What is wrong dear, any problem?' Monalisa continued asking.

'I lost maaa...my book. It was stolen together wii... with my wrist watch yeee... ye yesterday,' replied Usher as he stammered with an innocent look.

'What!' the class startled.

'Who can that be?' Liam whispered to Timothy.

'Did anyone see Usher's stuff?' the teacher asked with a very calm voice.

'Maybe he left them home,' replied Jolene one of the pupils in the classroom.

'No... no, they are not at home,' Usher hurried in to speak.

'They went missing from here,' Usher added.

Madam Monalisa asked the pupils to resurface Usher's book and watch before she started going over one by one to find them.

Everyone was asked to stand up, the teacher started checking. She started inspecting from the left column. Liam and the friends were in the middle column. After being checked from head to toe with your bag, you were asked to sit.

The teacher reached the middle column. Liam and the friends were sitting on the first row. She checked Timothy's bag and couldn't find anything. Anita's bag was checked too and there was nothing. On checking Liam and Sonia's bags, the watch and the book were found.

'How dare you take what doesn't belong to you?' asked the teacher furiously.

'I know this was a trick...' Sonia rushed in to speak.

'Keep quiet, just move to the office,' the teacher commanded angrily.

The entire class was horrified by what they had just witnessed.

'How can this be?' Anita whispered to Timothy.

'I can't tell,' Timothy replied.

No one believed that Liam and Sonia would do such an act.

Liam and Sonia headed to the staff room as the teacher had commanded.

'Liam, I am trying to figure out how this happened,' Sonia said with a puzzled look on her face.

The teacher continued with the lesson till the bell was sounded.

Anita and Timothy felt helpless because of what had happened to their friends.

'Your friends are going to be suspended,' Usher said happily.

'Watch your tongue dude,' Timothy replied pinpointing at Usher.

'Tell me you planned this slander you prick,' Anita talked furiously into Usher's face.

'Haha, me telling you the whole truth won't change a thing,' replied Usher mockingly.

Anita wanted to fight Usher but Timothy stopped him.

'A girl cannot fight me,' Usher added proudly.

'Stupid boy,' Anita said. Slapped Usher in the face and barged him.

'Go report me too,' Anita added as she rushed out of the class. She went behind the classroom block and she helplessly wept bitterly.

'So, you are thieves?' the teacher asked Liam and Sonia.

'It's not true teacher, perhaps someone put those items in our bags,' Liam said pleadingly.

'I won't listen to any of you, you are to be suspended for two weeks,' Monalisa said

'You very well know that theft is against the school rules and regulations,' she added.

'What! no Madam Monalisa please,' Sonia begged in a timid broken voice. She started crying.

'Please forgive us, mummy will not like this,' she added as the teacher stared at both of them.

'Since this is happening for the first time, you are to serve a punishment for at least one week,' suggested the teacher.

'You are obliged to tide up the library this entire week, if this happens again you will not only be suspended but also expelled from school for such habits are prohibited in school,' the teacher added oddly.

Monalisa asked both of them to return to class. Some pupils were having small talks, laughing at them calling them thieves.

'That's the cost of coming from deprived families,' Usher mocked as he by passed Liam and Sonia. They both never replied.

After classes, they couldn't make it to Pollah's house since they had to abide by what the teacher had instructed. Timothy and Anita elucidated the incident to Pollah when they reached there. She never liked what the little boy Usher had done.

'What is that boy's name?' Pollah asked.

'Usher,' Timothy answered.

Pollah sympathized with them, requested Timothy and Anita to pass on her greetings unto Liam and Sonia anytime they see them again and also guide them through what was discussed the whole week in their absentia.

'But who did this to us if not Usher?' Sonia asked Liam.

'I guess you are right it was his slanderous plan, remember when he lied about the teacher calling us, that was the time he did all his crap,' Liam replied.

'He will one day have to pay for this,' Sonia added as she mopped the Library tables.

Unfortunately, Usher's plan of getting the two friends suspended was not successful. The more he tried all the imprudent plans and failed, the more his resentment for the four friends got to the climax.

What these four friends used as a weapon to fail Usher was the widow's advice to stay calm and distance themselves from Usher. They never minded about what said or did to them. After the punishment week, Liam and Sonia rejoined the team for daily coaching.

# 16

A month later, the timetable for end of term exams was pinned out on the notice board. It was well indicated on the same notice board that after the exams, the school was to hold an exhibition day where different schools around the county were to participate in competitions of academics, Music, Dance and Drama etc.

All the pupils read harder to see that they could get good grades and get promoted to new classes at the end of the academic year. Liam and the group did all that was needed to make them pass the exams. Pollah too had their back.

On the day of the examinations the four friends passed by the widow' house, she gave them courage, prayed with them and wished them success in their exams. They walked to school ready for the exam. At exactly 9:00am the question papers were distributed. When Liam got the examination paper, he remembered what Pollah had told them.

'Remember what Pollah told us, pray before you do anything,' Liam whispered to Anita. Smiled.

All pupils started writing the exam as soon as the starting bell was sounded. No inconveniences were encountered throughout the examination session. They all handed in the exam papers to the teacher when the finishing bell was sounded.

The role of marking the examination papers started immediately. End of year examination marking usually consumed six calendar days and then results were always displayed on the school notice board for the entire school to see. The school general assembly was held on the following day after the six examination marking days. Best five students from each class were to be awarded and appreciated for their academic efforts and also as a motivation for the rest of the students to strive harder for better grades.

Friday afternoon, the bell for gathering at the assembly ground was sounded. Both the student's body and the school staff members came together.

The school headmaster Mr. Walter Kayemba opened up the speeches, he started with greeting the audience, thanked both pupils and teachers for the tremendous job done during the entire academic year and he then proceeded with reading out the agenda of the day.

'It was a remarkable year I must say, without wasting time, I will allow the class teachers of every class to announce to us the best performers,' he concluded as he passed the microphone to Mrs. Elaine Moraa, the class teacher to Junior class one (J.1)

She read out the names of pupils from her class, the next teacher also did the same till it was time to hear from Madam Emerald the class teacher of J.4. All the pupils from J.4 were curious, ready to know how they had performed.

'There has been a very great improvement in my class,' she started.

'Once I read your name, please come upfront for your present and report card,' she added.

The 1st pupil was Liam.

The 2nd pupil was Anita.

The 3rd pupil was Usher.

the 4th pupil was Timothy.

The 5th pupil was Sonia.

All the pupils from J.4 were shocked.

'Usher the 3rd!! Unbelievable,' pupils murmured.

Liam and the rest of the best performers were rewarded and given their report cards. Liam hugged Anita, he couldn't believe that he had finally made it.

Timothy couldn't believe it, he remembered his previous performance, he was the 23rd last year, Anita the 16th and Sonia the 27th. It was a huge improvement indeed.

After all the teachers were done with reading out the best performers, Mr. Sheldon Kwagala the Dean of Students (DoS) remined the students' body about the exhibition and what was expected that day.

'This doesn't mark the end of the term, we still have an exhibition which is in two weeks' time,' the DoS said.

'Remember the competition involves different schools from the county and the best school will win the trophy,' he added

'Kindly inform your parents early enough so that they can prepare for the day too. You need to come along with them,' the DoS concluded.

Liam, Sonia, Timothy and Anita rushed to rushed to the widow's house immediately after the school assembly.

'We made it,' they all shouted loudly. Cackled.

Pollah was amused after seeing their report cards.

'This is interesting,' she said as she perused through Liam's report card.

'Thanks, Aunt Pollah,' Timothy thanked the widow on behalf of others.

'We couldn't have made it without you,' he added

'Oh, before we forget, we are having an exhibition two weeks from now and you are invited,' Liam said.

'Wow, I will be glad to attend,' Pollah replied.

'We too will be happy to see you there Aunt Pollah,' Anita added.

'Let us have a toast for the exciting report cards,' suggested Pollah.

She picked lemonade from the fridge and poured into the glasses.

'Cheers,' they all said out loud as they toasted their glasses with a duchenne laughter.

'Mummy, can you believe this!' Liam exclaimed as he showed her the report card to her mother.

'You're the 1st, what!' Liam's mother exclaimed too as she stood up with the report card in her hands. Stared at the report card in total shock.

'Tell me this is true darling,' she added.

'Yes, Mum,' Liam replied with a broad smile.

'God job son, I am proud of you,' added the mother as she carried Liam high in the air.


## 17

Monday morning, Emerald came to class and requested the pupils to suggest what each of them would prefer to participate in during the exhibition competitions. They were tasked to make research, rehearse and also practice whatever they had chosen. A piece of paper was passed around the class where each pupil was to write their names and the choices made.

Liam and Usher selected academic discussions about maths and science respectively, Anita selected dancing, Sonia selected singing whereas Timothy selected playing a piano. Emerald declared the start of the practice and rehearsal week.

Liam had a plan for his group.

'Let's go seek help from Pollah,' Liam suggested.

They all agreed and later in the evening, they went to Pollah and explained to her on the fields they were to participate in. They explained to her what kind of support they needed this time around.

Luckily enough, Gabriel the late son of this Pollah owned a small piano which Timothy used for his practice and rehearsal.

Pollah had kept audio tapes of Jevelle's favorite songs from which Sonia picked the best song to practice. She further gave Anita video clips for her watch and imitate the good dance moves.

Everyone was occupied by the exhibition rehearsals. As it is always said that experience comes with time, it took a while for all of them of perfectionize. Other school pupils used to go to the school premises for rehearsals but the four friends stayed at Pollah's. The more they practiced and rehearsed, the more perfect their work turned out. Pollah tried everything possible to see to it that they could come out with the most unique presentation.

24 hours before the exhibition, the four friends went to the widow's home to remind her of big event. They asked her to come as early as she could so they would introduce her to their parents.

On the exhibition day, parents of different pupils came and also various schools had already arrived. The entire school main hall was full to its maximum. Anita, Sonia and Timothy arrived as early as they could, smartly dressed in their school uniforms together with their parents.

'Where is Pollah?' Liam asked Sonia as he looked through the crowd.

'I think she is on her way,' Sonia answered.

Hardly had they talked about her when she arrived smartly dressed in a red dress with a black blazer and black high heels.

'She is over there,' Liam said happily as he located Pollah by his fingers. They both rushed to where she was to welcome her. Pollah looked a little bit nervous because of the crowd.

'Good morning Aunt Pollah and thanks for coming,' Sonia said as she smiled

'You look smart,' Sonia commented as she observed Pollah from head to toe.

Around 9:00am, Mr. Walter Kayemba the school headmaster opened up the function by welcoming all parents and all schools that had arrived. The agenda

71

of the day was read out and all protocols that were to be followed that day.

Discussions were held first. Discussants from various schools discussed first, High Grade School representatives discussed last. Usher discussed before Liam.

When discussing, Liam looked through the audience to see if Pollah and his mother were observing him clearly. His discussion about algebra was very clear, educative and interactive. He left no stone unturned during his session and indeed he did all he could to present the best performance. He concluded the discussion by thanking the audience for their participation and attention. The audience appreciated his presentation with a loud applause. The entire audience got to their feet as a sign of gratitude to Liam.

'Wow,' Liam said to himself in a low note with an amused face.

The dancing competition followed. Representatives from other schools presented first. Anita finally came on stage to present 'Bailando by Enrique Iglesias' one of the famous Spanish singers. Her dance moves impressed everyone and almost the entire crowd sang along the music rhythm as she showed off the good dances. seeing Pollah and her mother in the audience gave her more passion and confidence.

Timothy came on stage to present his piano keys. He played 'we got love by the late Don Williams' He sang along as he played the entire song on his piano. He presented such a nice performance.

Sonia too showed up on the stage to sing. Her mother and siblings were watching. She with her melodious and angelic voice she presented 'You still the one by Shania Twain.

The competitions continued until all the performances were completed. Pupils presented poems, written articles, fashion and design, modelling etc.

The chief judge Mr. Hudson Lule came in with the final results.

'Good afternoon, everyone,' he greeted the audience.

'Thanks for turning up in large number as well continuing to stay here till this time, I am here to announce the best participants in today's competition,' he added with a winning smile.

'Kindly come upfront together with your parent once I call out your name,' he concluded.

The entire audience was as silent as a grave, they were all looking forward to listening from the judge.

Liam Magezi the son of Mr. and Mrs. Magezi was read as the best discussant. The audience clapped as Liam together with his mother and father walked up front. Liam was shocked on seeing his dad. It had been seven months without seeing each other due to the misunderstandings between Liam's parents. He was so happy to see his parents together again.

Anita Mirembe the daughter of Mr. and Mrs. Mirembe was called up front as the best dancer. The audience clapped as they moved forward.

Sonia Mulungi a daughter of Mr. and Mrs. Mulungi was announced the best singer. The audience clapped as she and her parents moved to the front.

Timothy Kirabo son of Mr. and Mrs. Kirabo was announced as the best instrumental competitor. Together with his parents, they walked to the front.

The announcements continued till all the best participants in different fields were read out. They were all rewarded with presents.

Finally, High Grade Junior School was announced the best school amongst all.

Liam was called upon to give a speech on behalf of the winning school.

Pollah watched everything and she looked happy.

'Good afternoon everyone, we are so glad that this exhibition has been a success. Thanks to whoever has participated, different schools that have given in a hand and everybody who has matched efforts so that this is a success,' Liam said

I am glad that our school High Grade Junior School emerged the best in this competition. I want to wish everyone a safe journey as we return to our homes. Thanks once again,' He concluded as he passed the microphone back unto the chief judge.

'Oh sorry, I have something to add,' Liam said as he asked for the microphone again.

'There is someone special I would like to introduce to you. She is the reason as to why me and my fellow competitors managed to emerge the best. She is really a good kind-hearted person. We regard her as our mother because indeed she treats us like one. All we presented today were her ideas and efforts combined.

'Aunt Pollah can I request you come and join us too please,' said Liam happily.

Sonia, Timothy and Anita clapped harder. They moved to where she was sitting to escort her to the front. The audience clapped as they all walked.

'Say something Aunt Pollah,' Liam requested the widow.

'Thank you darling, (paused a bit) thanks my children,' said Pollah. Eyes watered with a nervous look.

'Good afternoon ladies and gentlemen plus the students' body at large,' she greeted the crowd.

'Aaa... these are the ones I call my children (rubbed off tears). Most of you know what happened to my family. Life with Sonia, Liam, Anita and Timothy feels complete, turned to look at Liam and the fellows, you are all that I call children,' Pollah spoke with a timid broken voice. Liam held her hand from the right side and Timothy from the left side.

The audience pitied her, some of the parents were seen wiping tears from their eyes because of the terrible memory.

'You are loved and thank you for everything Aunt Pollah,' Sonia said after Pollah passed back the microphone to the organizer.

'Just one last point before we all depart, Liam will be our new appointed head prefect come next year,' the headmaster announced.

'Thank you all for coming, go in peace,' he concluded and closed the exhibition after the closing prayer was said. Everyone planned on leaving the school premises.

Liam, Anita, Sonia and Timothy introduced Pollah to their parents.

'Thanks Miss. Pollah, sorry about your loss,' said Elsy Liam's mother. Shook hands with her.

'I have heard a lot about you,' added Gianne Sonia's mother. They all laughed.

The four friends requested their parents' permission to go with Pollah then return home later on. Fortunately, the parents accepted.

'Pollah, thanks again,' Sonia said. Smiled.

'We are coming with you,' Timothy said. Intrigued.

They moved to Pollah's house. Conversed all through the way to the house.

On reaching home, Pollah swiftly walked to her bedroom for a refreshment leaving the four friends in the sitting room watching telly. They cooked up a plan, guess what it was?

'Let's give all our trophies to her,' suggested Anita.

'Yes, that's a great idea,' Liam said.

They whispered to each other planning on what to do and how to do it. When they heard Pollah returning to the sitting room, they all pretended like nothing was happening.

'Aunt Pollah, we got you a gift,' Liam said. They all smiled at each other.

'What is it my lovies?' she asked curiously.

The four friends stood up and gave their exhibition trophies to her.

'Take them, they belong to you that's all your effort Aunt Pollah,' Timothy said.

Pollah couldn't believe it. She burst into tears as she hugged them all together.

'Thanks, my little ones,' said Pollah. She wiped off the tears.

'We are your children now and forever,' Sonia said.

The affectionate widow's life wholly changed, she had no more woe as she had before.

# 18

A week down the road, Pollah planned to take the four friends for a trip in Zanzibar but she had to consult their parents before anything else. They were to travel by bus.

Zanzibar is an island in the southern part of Tanzania known for its good Masai culture, good blue waters, beaches, resorts and several other tourist attractions.

She reached out to the parents and they all agreed. She worked out all the costs for the trip including transport, accommodation, feeding, shopping etc.

She told them about the pan and she further asked them to inform their parents who packed clothes, shoes, bags and everything else that was needed

Saturday morning, they all woke up very early in the morning. Moved to the bus park boarded and went off. The entire group was so happy, Pollah sat midst the four with Anita and Sonia on the right then Liam and Timothy on the left.

'Someone tell us a gripping story,' Pollah said. Smiled broadly.

'I can do it, I have one,' Sonia reacted swiftly.

'Please go on if it's not the one of the lions in the jungle,' Timothy said.

'Give her time to prepare herself,' Liam added. Roared the whole group. They laughed noisily in that the other passengers turned to just see what the matter was.

Sonia commenced narrating the story. It was about the cruel dad. Pollah and the others were attentively listening to the story.

'That was my story,' Sonia concluded after telling the entire story. Sighed.

'Thanks, Sonia,' said Pollah. Passed her fingers in Sonia's hair.

'It was a good one,' Anita added looking delighted.

'To me, it sounded so imprudent.' Liam said. Laughed hoarsely.

Sonia looked pissed about what the latter friend had said.

'It's a jive, come on,' Liam said as he poked Sonia. The group narrated as many stories as they would since the journey was a bit longer.

'I feel hungry and sleepy,' Timothy yawned while talking. He really looked exhausted.

'Don't worry, we are about to reach our destination,' Pollah comforted him.

Midday, they had reached Zanzibar.

'Wow! this is a great city,' Liam exclaimed. Stared at the skyscraper and the busy streets.

They made a row of five with everyone holding each other's hand. Strolled through the city up to Elewana's Kilindi Resort where they were to spend the trip.

Pollah rushed to the entrance, picked entrance tickets for the four friends.

'Come on let's go enjoy,' Said Pollah. Pulled the row towards the entrance. The whole group laughed. They paced to the beach shores. The place was surrounded by multitudes of people enjoying their holidays.

'I will go swimming,' Liam said.

'Me for swinging and volley ball and...' said Anita.

'Volley ball! You are too young for that,' Sonia said. Stared at Anita.

'Me I will go for...,' Sonia spoke in beats.

'Ok let's go now,' The widow suggested.

'My swimming wear, I can't find it,' Liam said in a baffled voice. Pollah helped him find it in his bag. Liam put on the wear and dived into the beach waters.

'Don't go far Liam, you may drown,' echoed Pollah.

Anita went for swinging on the pendulum as Sonia played in the sand with other children from different countries and families.

'Timothy, what about you darling?' the widow asked.

'Well, I am still making up my mind to come up with the best choice, I am always unique you know that,' Timothy said. Guffawed.

'I will rush in for football,' Said Timothy. He ran to the other side where football was being played.

'That's what children do,' Sighed Pollah. She rested on the seats under the grass thatched hut alongside the beach waters. She watched the four friends playing. Her eyes kept on moving from direction to direction. She looked anteriorly to check on Liam in the beach waters, Anita and Sonia on the left side and Timothy on the right side. She couldn't rest her neck because she had to supervise all the children to make sure that nothing bad happened to them.

'Good afternoon madam,' greeted a foreign woman. Sat by Pollah's right hand side.

'Good afternoon too ma'am,' Pollah replied. Smiled faintly.

They all looked at each other and smiled.

The woman seemed to be in her late 30s dressed in a pink short dress with a brown ribbon in her braided hair.

'Is that your son?' asked the woman pointing at Liam busy swimming in the beach waters. Pollah looked blank for a moment.

'Ye... yeah,' she replied in a broken voice.

'He is a nice boy,' the woman added.

'I am Amber,' she introduced herself to Pollah.

They introduced themselves to each other and also discussed. Hardly had they started discussing more when Sonia came running to Pollah complaining of hunger.

'Oh dear, call upon your other fellows so that we can go have lunch,' said Pollah. Checked her wrist watch to establish the time.

'At exactly 2:00pm, you shall resume with your playing,' she added.

Sonia ran fast to call the others so that they would go for lunch.

'What of her?' Amber asked Pollah.

'They are four and they are all my children,' replied the widow confidently.

'You have beautiful children,' the woman said. She then turned to her right only to see the four friends walking to where they were sitting. She smiled.

'I was still enjoying,' Timothy said with a sad face.

'Sorry, but we have to eat something,' Pollah comforted Timothy.

'Remember when I told you about greeting all strangers that come our way,' added Pollah.

'We are so sorry Aunt Pollah,' Liam pleaded on behalf of others.

'I am Anita, he is Liam, he is Timothy and she is Sonia,' replied Anita as she pointed to each one of them.

'Oh, you have good names,' Amber said. Smiled.

'Please, we would like to know your name too,' Timothy humbly asked.

'I am Mrs. Amber Kirabo,' replied the woman.

'Wow! She is Kirabo too, my name sake!' exclaimed Timothy.

They all laughed in a group.

'Let's go for lunch then,' Pollah said. She stood up, joined the four friends as they moved to the beach hotel leaving Mrs. Amber Kirabo alone in the chair.

'Bye Mrs. Kirabo,' the group waved.

They entered the hotel, it was a palatial, cool and cozy with South African local music playing. The waiter approached them and displayed the menu cards.

'Yes, I want beef with rice,' Timothy said.

'I prefer deep fried fish with chips,' Anita hurried in to say.

Liam ordered for chicken and rice, Sonia for Irish potatoes, Pollah for rice with mushroom soup and green vegetables. They later ordered for soft drinks.

'The fish tastes exactly like what mum prepared on my birthday,' Anita said with her mouth full of food.

'Eat as much as you can because you are playing till very late in the evening and the entire week too. The widow said as she cleaned her lips with a paper towel.

'I am extremely satisfied, I won't play well now,' Sonia said as she passed her palms on her belly.

The entire group laughed at her. The four friends resumed playing until they were all exhausted. Around 6pm, they were all tired not even one of them requested for more playing.

They moved to the hotel room, showered and changed into their night wears, walked down stairs to the restaurant for dinner in the same hotel after then moved to their rooms to sleep. As they walked, Anita noticed a place where people were seated surrounding the burning fire.

'What's that Aunt Pollah?' Sonia asked.

'It's called a fire place,' Pollah answered.

'Wow I have added that to my vocabulary,' Sonia spoke as she smiled.

They proceeded to where they were to sleep busy conversing.

'I am frightened sleeping alone,' Anita said with her arms crossed in the chest.

'Shame upon you Anita,' Sonia said imitating Anita.

'Stop it Sonia,' Pollah said.

'Anita darling come sleep in my bed,' she added.

'Good night everyone,' Liam said. Rushed to bed.

Early in the morning, they all woke up, prayed as a group, showered went for breakfast. They did the playing for the rest of the days.

On Sunday morning, they boarded back home.

'It was really a good one, we enjoyed ourselves,' Liam said. Leant on the bus seat.

'I really enjoyed, I will write this moment in my diary,' Sonia said. Looked at Pollah.

Timothy was seen dozing perhaps of the much exhaustion.

'My goodness! Timothy stop dozing please,' Anita exclaimed. Pulled his white t-shirt.

'Do you know what, you look like a wild duck when dozing,' Anita added.

Timothy opened his eyes.

'Leave me alone Anita. It's a jet lag,' Timothy said hoarsely.

'Jet lag! This is not a plane Timothy come on,' Liam Cackled.

The entire group was convulsed with and dissolved in laughter.

Pollah was listening to what the children were discussing. She showed amazement though at times sunk into deep thoughts.

The kids enjoyed the trip and all that came along with it.

In the evening, they were back home. Strikingly, all their parents were waiting for them at the bus park.

'Welcome back,' Liam's mother said. Embraced the four friends.

'Who told that we were coming back today mummy?' Sonia asked her mother blissfully.

'Pollah notified us earlier,' Sonia's mother replied with smiles.

'Everyone is returning home, we shall meet some other moment,' Pollah said with her arms behind.

'No, come with us please,' Sonia pleaded naughtily.

'Come to me my dear,' Pollah called upon Sonia (made signs of calling her.) Sonia rushed to where she was.

Pollah squatted to meet Sonia's height.

'Time will come for me to come to your house,' she added.

'I can't wait for that time to arrive,' Sonia replied.

All the parents were so impressed by the way Pollah treated their children. They watched the strong bond between the kids and the widow. They all walked to their respective homes. Pollah too moved to hers.

'I enjoyed myself mummy,' Liam elucidated to his mother.

'Pollah bought us good meals,' he added.

'She did good,' Liam's mother replied.

'Please have some rest, you look so tired,' Elsy said.

# 19

One week after the trip, the four friends planned to ask permission from their parents to go spend the rest of the holiday with Pollah.

They explained the whole plan to Pollah and they asked her to help talk to their parents too. Due to the good and sheer coincidence, the parents accepted. The four friends shifted to Pollah's house as soon as the proposal was granted.

'You are to use this room,' said the widow pointing at the late Gabriel's room. That was told to Timothy and Liam. Anita and Sonia were to use the late Jevelle's room.

'Well, since I fear darkness, then Sonia will protect me,' Anita said. Sat on the bed.

Pollah gave me a quick orientation around the place.

'What is that?' Timothy asked pointing at a tricycle in the corner of the store.

'It was Gabriel's tricycle,' The widow replied.

'Can I play with it?' Timothy asked sharply.

'Yes, my darling but you will have to share it with Liam,' the widow replied.

Anita and Sonia looked at each other in a puzzle.

'So, we are left out?' Sonia asked.

'No please, you and Anita will play with the dolls that belonged to Jevelle. Pollah explained. Stared at them.

'Feel at home, this is your other home,' said the widow as she moved down the staircases.

They all sat in the sitting room. Sonia looked un settled. She looked side to side.

'Sonia feels at home,' She whispered to herself.

They prepared lunch, ate and did all house work together. Anita and Sonia helped wash utensils while Timothy and Liam helped clean the compound and sitting room.

'I feel very comfortable whenever am with this woman. She is more like my mother,' Timothy told Liam. They both laughed.

'Not you alone, I guess everyone of us feels the same way,' replied Liam.

Time passed when the four friends are still in Pollah's home. They all had a marvelous time at the widow's place.

On the last day at Pollah's, the widow had prepared a striking idea for the friends.

'Liam, Anita, Timothy and Sonia come on. I have something for you,' Pollah called the four friends. They came swiftly to hear what the matter was. (Beats of silence.)

'What is it Pollah?' Sonia asked on behalf of others. They all looked curious.

'Is it about returning home?' Liam asked looking startled. The widow smiled.

'Please go make yourselves ready we are going for shopping because this is the last day you staying here, you are resuming school soon.' Pollah answered.

'Certainly!' Anita exclaimed. Rushed to her room to change her dress.

The entire group dressed up nicely and drove off to town. In the supermarket, Liam and the group picked all that they needed.

'Pick whatever you like,' The widow said to the group.

Liam picked a toy gun, snickers, ice cream and other things. Anita picked dolls and shoes. Timothy picked baseball boots, baseball caps and a watch. Sonia picked a bangle and beret.

'We are done,' Liam said.

'Sure, that's not enough I guess.' Pollah said. Smiled

'Let me pick more for you,' she added.

Moved to the first floor of the supermarket. She picked more things for the kids, among all the things she chose, there were four lockets and four school bags.

When they reached home, Pollah went to her bedroom, checked inside her wallet and got the small sized wallet photos she had obtained from the trip they had in Zanzibar and placed each one's photo into the lockets.

'This is my gift for you,' She said as she reached the sitting room.

Gave them their respective lockets and a bag each.

'Wow! They look good,' Timothy exclaimed. He put on this bag and the locket.

'Keep it with you, that's my gift for you,' the widow added.

In the evening, the widow dropped each of them back to their respective homes. She wished them a good new school term. Their parents were very happy to see their children back.

Monday morning, it was school new term. They all went to school with not only the nice-looking lockets but also similar bags. All the pupils at school stared at the four friends. They entered class with all eyes on them.

'Welcome back from the long holiday,' Sonia said to the class. Moved to her seat.

Their English teacher Mr. Heizer Kagame, came in, greeted the class and welcomed them from the long holiday.

'Today we are to introduce ourselves to a new sub topic which is story writing,' the teacher added. Wrote the topic on the chalkboard.

'You are to write about any good event you saw or heard during the holiday,' He added as he walked around the class. She taught them how to make nice and interesting stories. Different pupils were called upon to tell stories to the class on the interesting things they saw during the holiday. This was done until the end of the lesson.

'That's all I had for you, please go write your stories. I will need to look at them tomorrow,' the teacher concluded. Matched out of the class.

'I suppose we write about our trip,' Liam suggested.

'That's a great idea,' Anita said as she pulled out her book from the new bag.

The four friends made stories about the trip they had. Pollah as usual guided them on how to do it best.

The next morning, the teacher came back to class and asked Usher to collect all the story books from the pupils.

'I hope you wrote nice and interesting stories,' he said.

He marked the stories and gave marks accordingly. That very evening she came to class back with the pupil's books.

'You tried making good stories, I was really impressed,' he said.

The whole class was quiet just waiting for the best story writer.

'Liam, Anita, Sonia and Timothy wrote on the same topic but they did it well. Liam wrote the best story,' Heizer said.

'Keep practicing on how to write impressive stories.' The teacher concluded, he then moved out of the class.

Liam had made it another time. Usher was behind burning of anger. Usher never liked Liam's progress.

'You fool, let it not happen this term again, you are my worst nightmare,' Usher said, spat on Liam then moved out.

'It's no big deal Usher, do everything you wanna do,' Liam sadly echoed to Usher who had reached the class veranda. The other pupils Cackled.

What bothered Usher was that Liam was being talked about by almost all the teachers yet he wanted to always be him.

The following day, more topics were given out, for pupils to compose stories on. They all had to come out with different versions. In all the story writings, Liam performed best.

In his last story, Liam wrote about the unruly king, unfortunately Usher copied his work and presented it to the teacher first. He wanted to be the best this round.

'Usher and Liam, how come you have the same work,' the teacher asked.

'That thief copied my work.' Usher hurried in to speak as he stammered.

Liam had nothing to say, he remained silent.

'It's him who copied my work teacher,' Liam tried defending himself.

'It's you Liam,' Usher replied back, pinpointing at him.

The class had turned into a court since the arguing was much. It was like two leopards fighting.

'Stupid boy, thief, I hate you so much,' Usher said angrily.

'Stop it, Usher why do you use such word in such a small matter,' move out of my class. I want to find you in the staff room.' The teacher loudly said. Usher was chased out of the class because of the bad manners he had portrayed.

Usher's manners worsened day by day as those of Liam became better every day. The more the teachers loved Liam the more Usher hated him.

Being the appointed head prefect as per the head master last year, Liam was told to address the school on the first welcome back school assembly gathering. He advised the pupils to portray discipline in everything they do, read hard and to also love each other. He was asked the pupils respect tears and always behave well

'Take me as an example, at least behave like me,' Liam said jokingly.

The entire school audience laughed.

Usher was at the back looking red. He couldn't bear the situation.

'That would be me standing there,' Usher said to himself. His eyes watered.

'My friends Anita, Timothy, Sonia, Enock and... Usher plus the entire school community I love you all,' Liam concluded.

He returned the microphone to the head teacher and moved back to his seat.

'He spoke about Usher!' Anita exclaimed. All Junior Class 5 pupils were so surprised on hearing what Liam had said about Usher for they knew about their impaired relationship. After the assembly, Usher immediately rushed to Liam looking indignant.

'So, you put shame unto me in front of the whole school, publicizing me as your friend, am not your friend, I don't like you and never will I, nothing can ever explain you, you imperative creature,' Usher insulted Liam. He pushed him and he fell down by his back. Geared and moved away.

Liam never said anything in return. He stood up and walked away. Most of the pupils were watching what had happened. Majority didn't like Usher's reaction.

'What will you do to come out of his resentment?' Sonia asked Liam.

'Leave that, I will find a way of fixing it. I will put everything to right,' Liam said in a low tone.

They moved to class to pick their bags and go home. Liam was hurt about the words Usher said. The words kept on echoing in his ears.

'I will have to talk to Usher,' Liam said to himself.

The following day in the evening, Liam called Usher behind the library block for a brief conversation.

'What is wrong with you, idiot?' Usher asked. Eyes widely open.

'Usher I am not here to insult you. I just want to tell you that all you are doing is not right,' Liam said.

'Hahaha, not right! Is that the reason why you called me here?' Usher asked. Laughed in mockery.

'Please Usher listen to me, I have no problem with you. Change the way you treat me,' Liam pleaded.

'If it's about my improvement in class, I can help you please but stop insulting me, it hurts,' Liam added.

Usher looked straight into Liam's eyes and said,

'I need nothing from you. Just get lost.' geared and moved away.

Liam remained standing alone. He started crying because Usher failed to understand his point of view.

'Oh God,' sighed Liam, leant against the library block.

Weeks passed with Usher's harsh treatment to Liam. Usher did all that was possible to make Liam look a bad boy, he ashamed him every time he found him. Despite all the acts, Liam kept his head on to the extent that he got used to the way Usher used to treat him

Usher lost his friends just because of his bad habits. All teachers started complaining about what Usher had turned himself into.

After a period of one month and half, seeing that Liam wasn't responding to all the provokes he made, Usher came to Liam asking for forgiveness.

'I am so sorry Liam, I accept not to snub you again,' Usher said.

'I have nothing against you Usher,' replied Liam in total shock

'Aunt Pollah told me that hate never drives out hate, its love that does,' he said

'I told you, I will always be waiting for your decision,' Liam added. They embraced each other for the first time.

'I forgive you Usher,' he added.


# 20

Few days later, the class got to know about the reconciliation between Usher and Liam.

'Usher is now our new friend,' Liam told Anita, Timothy and Sonia.

'Liam, not Usher, he treated us ill. He is a bad boy, so indisciplined, he said he hates us, remember the day he lied that we had stolen his book and watch,' Sonia said angrily.

'Liam, I can't associate myself with evil people like him.' Sonia added. She walked away in total anger.

Liam ran after her so that he could explain. He managed to convince Sonia and brought her back.

'Forget that Sonia, am really sorry,' Usher said humbly.

'Don't ever call my name again, I am not talking to you,' Sonia replied. Tears rolled down her cheeks.

'People like you don't deserve forgiveness,' she added as she cried bitterly

'Liam may forget but I will never forget all that you did to us you evil boy, you have never loved us Usher. Beefing and hating us for no reason. But ww...h... why?' Sonia concluded. Burst into tears.

'Shameless boy, I can't accept you as my friend,' Anita also said.

'If we are to forgive you, you will have to apologize to us mainly Liam,' Timothy suggested.

'I accept it all. I am sorry please,' Usher said.

The whole group moved away leaving Usher stranded. They went to Pollah's place and explained the whole situation to her.

'Should we forgive him Pollah?' Anita asked.

'Yes, my children forgive him and start a new chapter. Make him your friend too,' the widow said.

'But he is not worth forgiving and befriending,' Anita said.

'Anita, in life we should learn to forgive others because if we forgive we earn ourselves peace of mind,' Pollah added.

'I agree we can forgive him but never making him our friend,' Sonia said

The next day the four friends called Usher.

'We need to talk to you,' Anita said.

'We choose to forgive you, let this not happen again please,' Timothy added.

'Thanks, so much Liam. Am really sorry on all that happened. Am a new boy now. I really apologize,' Usher said. Looked so scared. He knelt before the four friends.

'Oh no Usher come on! Men don't kneel. Stand up buddy,' Liam said. Helped Usher to get to his feet.

Usher looked directly and strongly into Liam's eyes. Hugged him tightly for a minute. Tears came out of his eyes. Shook hands together. He couldn't believe that he had been forgiven.

After one week, the four friends took Usher to Pollah's house. She welcomed them as always.

'This is Usher, the one we told you about last time,' Liam introduced Usher.

Usher became a good friend to them. Pollah treated him like others despite all he had done to his fellows. She gave them new names (nick names). Liam was nicknamed 'rock star', Timothy 'pro guy', Sonia 'princess', Anita 'major domo', Usher 'prime star'. They lived happily and did everything together.

Pollah reunited them. A true affectionate widow, she loved them.

## THE END